GROUP SOUP

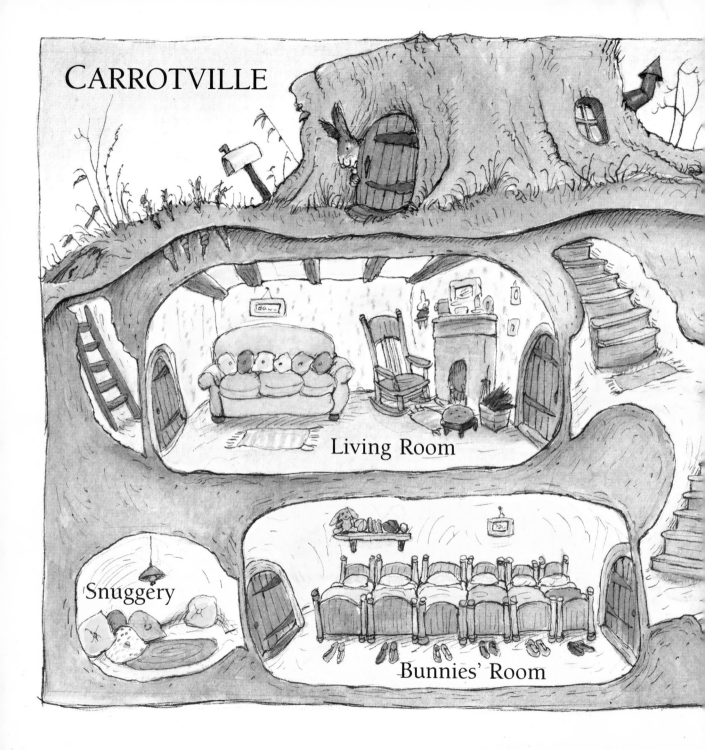

CARROTVILLE

Living Room

Snuggery

Bunnies' Room

Attic

Dining Room

Kitchen

Mama's
Room

Rhoda   Ricky   Mama   Margaret   Rowdy   Rooter   Rena
              Rabbit   Rose

GROUP SOUP

A BANK STREET BOOK ABOUT VALUES

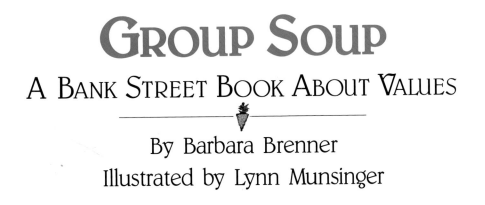

By Barbara Brenner

Illustrated by Lynn Munsinger

VIKING

VIKING
Published by the Penguin Group
Viking Penguin, a division of Penguin Books USA Inc.,
375 Hudson Street, New York, New York 10014, U.S.A.
Penguin Books Ltd, 27 Wrights Lane, London W8 5TZ, England
Penguin Books Australia Ltd, Ringwood, Victoria, Australia
Penguin Books Canada Ltd, 2801 John Street, Markham, Ontario, Canada L3R 1B4
Penguin Books (N.Z.) Ltd, 182-190 Wairau Road, Auckland 10, New Zealand

Penguin Books Ltd, Registered Offices: Harmondsworth, Middlesex, England

First published in 1992 by Viking Penguin, a division of Penguin Books USA Inc.

1 3 5 7 9 10 8 6 4 2

Series graphic design by Alex Jay/Studio J
Editor: Gillian Bucky
Special thanks to James A. Levine, William H. Hooks, and Regina Hayes

Copyright © Byron Preiss Visual Publications, Inc., 1992.

Text copyright © The Bank Street College of Education, 1992.

Illustrations copyright © Byron Preiss Visual Publications, Inc., and Lynn Munsinger, 1992.

A Byron Preiss Book

Carrotville is a trademark of The Bank Street College of Education.

Library of Congress Cataloging-in-Publication Data
Brenner, Barbara. Group soup / by Barbara Brenner ;
illustrated by Lynn Munsinger.   p.   cm.—(Carrotville ; no. 3)
Summary: A selfish rabbit learns that sharing is the one
ingredient needed to make the perfect Group Soup.
ISBN 0-670-82867-X
[1. Rabbits—Fiction. 2. Sharing—Fiction.] I. Munsinger, Lynn,
ill. II. Title. III. Series: Carrotville adventure ; no. 3.
PZ7.B7518Gr 1992 [E]—dc20   91-28862 CIP AC

Printed in Singapore

For Daniella – B.B.
For Molly – L.M.

Rhoda, Rena, Ricky, Rooter, Rowdy, and Margaret Rose were heading for home.

"I'm starving," said Rhoda. "I hope Mama made something good for dinner."

Margaret Rose always copied Rhoda. So now she said, "I'm starving, too. I could eat a whole turnip tart."

"I could eat two," said Ricky.

"Three," said Rena.

"Four," said Rooter. And Rowdy shouted, "Five!"

But Rhoda said she could eat seventeen turnip tarts. That's how hungry she was!

The six little rabbits scampered down the rabbit hole. But when they hopped into the kitchen, there was no welcome smell of cooking. There was only a note on the table. It said:

Dear Children:

Grandma Rabbit has the flu and I am hopping off to see her. You will have to make your own dinner. I'm sure that together you can cook something good.

Rhoda Rabbit groaned.

"No dinner! And I'm starving!"

She thumped one paw on the floor impatiently.

Ricky said, "I know how to make soup. Let's get started."

"Count me out. I'm too hungry to help," said Rhoda.

Ricky filled the big pot with water and put it on the stove. He added a pinch of salt and a dash of pepper.

"Now that's a good start," he said.

"Start for what?" asked Rhoda.

"For delicious soup," said Ricky.

"It doesn't look like soup," said Rhoda. "It looks like water."

"There is one thing it needs," said Ricky. "Every good soup needs a potato."

Rena pricked up her ears. She remembered the potato she was saving under her bed for a rainy day. "If all it needs is a potato, I know where to find one," she said.

Rena ran and got the potato.

Ricky peeled it and sliced it
and dropped it into the pot.
He stirred the soup and tasted it.
"Now we're getting somewhere," he said.
"Is it soup yet?" asked Rhoda in a cranky voice.

"Not quite yet," said Ricky. "It needs one more thing. A carrot," he announced. "It can't be soup without a sweet, crunchy carrot."

Rowdy's nose twitched. He had a carrot
hidden in the attic.

"If it really needs a carrot, I guess I could
find one," he said.

Rowdy brought the carrot to Ricky, who
scraped it and diced it and dropped it
into the pot.

"It's beginning to smell like soup," said Ricky.

"Yes, but is it soup? I can't eat the smell," snapped Rhoda.

"It's not quite soup yet," said Ricky. "Mama says soup should always have something green in it."

Rooter said, "I have some green beans in my backpack."

Soon Rooter's green beans were simmering in the pot with the carrot and potato.

"Ah, what a soup," said Ricky. But in the next breath he said, "Uh-oh! I forgot."

"Forgot what?" wailed Rhoda.

"Soup needs a turnip for luck. And I know just where to find one." He reached into his pocket. "I was saving this for a snack."

A few minutes went by.

"Now is it soup?" whined Rhoda.

"We're getting there," said Ricky.

"Mama always puts celery in soup," said Margaret Rose. "And I found some in the fridge."

"You're right, little sister," said Ricky. "Just what this soup needs."

"I think I just fainted from hunger," snarled Rhoda.

The soup smelled wonderful. The noses of the six rabbits twitched, and their tummies rumbled.

They watched anxiously as Ricky tasted
one more time.

"Hmmm," he muttered. "It's close. But
something is still missing."

"I don't believe this," groaned Rhoda.
She grabbed the spoon from
Ricky. "I'll taste it," she said.

Rhoda took a spoonful of soup.

She tasted Rena's potato...and she tasted Rowdy's carrot...Rooter's green beans... Ricky's turnip...Margaret Rose's celery. Yes, there *was* something missing.

Suddenly she knew what was missing. *She* was missing. She was the only one who hadn't helped with the soup!

"I know what it needs," she said. "This soup needs some parsley to sprinkle on top. And I know just where to find some."

Rhoda ran down to the snuggery. There was the pot of parsley she kept just for herself. She brought it back to the kitchen.

Snip, snip. She cut some fresh leaves of parsley into the soup.

"There," she said. "Now it's soup."

And they all sat down to eat.

"That was the best soup I ever ate," said Ricky.
"The very best," said Rena.
"Hear, hear," said Rowdy.
"Is there a name for this kind of soup?"
Rooter wanted to know.
Rhoda said, "I think we should call it
Group Soup, because everyone helped to make
it. Even a very hungry, cranky rabbit."
Rhoda Rabbit's ears twitched happily.

Rhoda made up a song:

Words by Rhoda

COUNT ME IN

Music by Lorenzo Martinez

It's great to be part of the group if
you're play-ing games or mak-ing soup. So
count me in. Don't count me out.
That's what shar-ing is all a-bout!